FAVOURITE CLASSICS
The Secret Garden

Retold by Sasha Morton
Illustrated by Andy Catling

An Hachette UK Company

www.hachette.co.uk

Copyright © Octopus Publishing Group Ltd 2013

First published in Great Britain in 2013 by TickTock,

an imprint of Octopus Publishing Group Ltd,

Endeavour House, 189 Shaftesbury Avenue,

London WC2H 8JY.

www.octopusbooks.co.uk

ISBN 978 1 84898 814 9

Printed and bound in China

10 9 8 7 6 5 4 3 2 1

With thanks to Lucy Cuthew

Contents

The Characters

Mary Lennox

Dickon

Colin Craven

Flowers from the garden

Mrs Medlock

Martha

The Robin

Ben Weatherstaff

Mr Craven

Chapter 1
India

Mary Lennox was born in luxury in India, but she did not get off to a good start in life.

She was a **sickly, grumpy** baby who became a **sickly, grumpy** toddler.

Mary was looked after by an Indian nanny, called an Ayah. The Ayah was instructed by Mary's parents not to let the child bother them and so by the time she was nine years old,

Mary was as selfish as any girl who had ever lived.

One hot morning, Mary awoke in a bad mood as usual. Her Ayah didn't come when she called and the servants seemed scared. Mary was left to play on her own all day.

A terrible fever called cholera had broken out. Mary hid away in the nursery and was forgotten about as one after another, the servants died or ran away.

8

Mary wept and slept the days away, until one morning she heard voices in the house.

"Why was I forgotten?"

Mary shouted at a man in the hallway. **"Why did nobody come?"**

"There was nobody left to come," said the man softly. And so Mary discovered that she was alone in the world.

Mary was being sent to live with her uncle,
Mr Craven, in England.

On the long sea voyage, Mary started to feel rather lonely.
Maybe in England she would belong to a family of her own.

Mary was met in London by a stern-looking woman called Mrs Medlock, who was the housekeeper at her uncle's home, a big country house called Misselthwaite Manor.

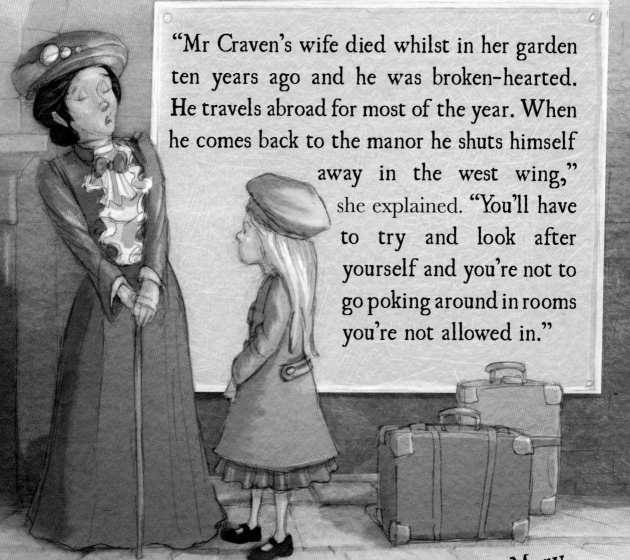

"Mr Craven's wife died whilst in her garden ten years ago and he was broken-hearted. He travels abroad for most of the year. When he comes back to the manor he shuts himself away in the west wing," she explained. "You'll have to try and look after yourself and you're not to go poking around in rooms you're not allowed in."

What a strange place England was, thought Mary.

Chapter 2
Misselthwaite Manor

After the long train journey, Mary and Mrs Medlock travelled by carriage to Misselthwaite Manor.

The wind howled across the wild, bleak moors.

Finally, they stopped at the only building for miles around. Mary looked up at the grand house with wide eyes. Mrs Medlock had told her that there were more than one hundred rooms inside. Most of them were kept locked, but there was a big garden for Mary to play in.

A light glowed in an upstairs window
and Mary nervously wondered
if this was her uncle's room.
Like it or not, Mary Lennox
was home.

When Mary looked out of her bedroom window on her very first morning at Misselthwaite Manor, all she could see was the endless, purple moor.

"Who is going to get me dressed?" asked Mary. She frowned at the servant who was in her room, in her usual, cross way.

"Can't you dress yourself?" said the maid in surprise.

"Of course not! My Ayah always did it for me," exclaimed Mary.

"Well, it's time you learned," said the maid firmly. The maid's name was Martha and she was a kind young woman.

Once Mary was dressed, the maid found her a coat and boots and showed her the way outside.

15

Martha had told Mary of a garden that was surrounded by high walls, which had been locked up by Mr Craven. After his wife had died, he had buried the key so no one could go inside.

Mary could not help wondering whether anything might be growing in this secret garden as she wandered around.

When she found an elderly ma[n] digging up vegetables she s[tood] next to him. **"Where is** [the] garden which belonged t[o] Mr Craven's wife?"

she asked.

T[...]
a[...]
n[...]
th[...]
tha[...]

Wit[...]
Mar[...]

Chapter 3
e Key

ed to look forward to

lthwaite Manor. She

e cheeks. Her eyes

w stronger.

Mary's favourite place to explore was the path around one of the walled gardens. She often noticed a cheerful little robin there and was envious of this bird. He was able to get inside the place she was sure was the secret garden.

But despite checking under the long curtains of ivy that grew over the wall, Mary could not find a way in.

One stormy day, Mary went
looking for the library and was
soon quite lost.

"I believe I have taken a
wrong turn," she whispered
to herself. "I don't know
which way to go now."

At that moment,
the silence was broken
by a cry. Mary gasped. She put
her hand on the tapestry in front of her.
To her surprise, it moved back to reveal a doorway.

Just then, Mrs Medlock found Mary and startled
her by shouting,
"What are you doing here?"

"I heard someone crying out," replied Mary.

"Nonsense! It was just the wind coming off the moors," said Mrs Medlock. "I'm taking you back to your room, right away!"

That night, Mary heard the crying sound again.

"Did you hear that?" she asked Martha.
"It sounded just like a child crying!"

Looking worried, Martha shook her head.
"It was just the wind," she said, but Mary knew that
Martha was lying to her, just like Mrs Medlock had.

The next morning, the storm had passed and the sun shone. Ben Weatherstaff was much more cheerful and called out, "Spring's coming!" to Mary.

"Do you think the robin knows if anything is growing in the secret garden?" asked Mary.

Ben replied gruffly, "Ask him. If anyone's been inside there this last ten years, he has."

Mary followed the robin to the garden's walls. Then she noticed he was pecking at one of the flower beds. Mary saw something half buried in the soil... **it was a key!**

Just then, a gust of wind blew some strands of ivy into the air and Mary saw a doorknob.

She turned the key in the rusty lock. Taking a deep breath, Mary pushed open the wooden door and slipped through it and into the secret garden…

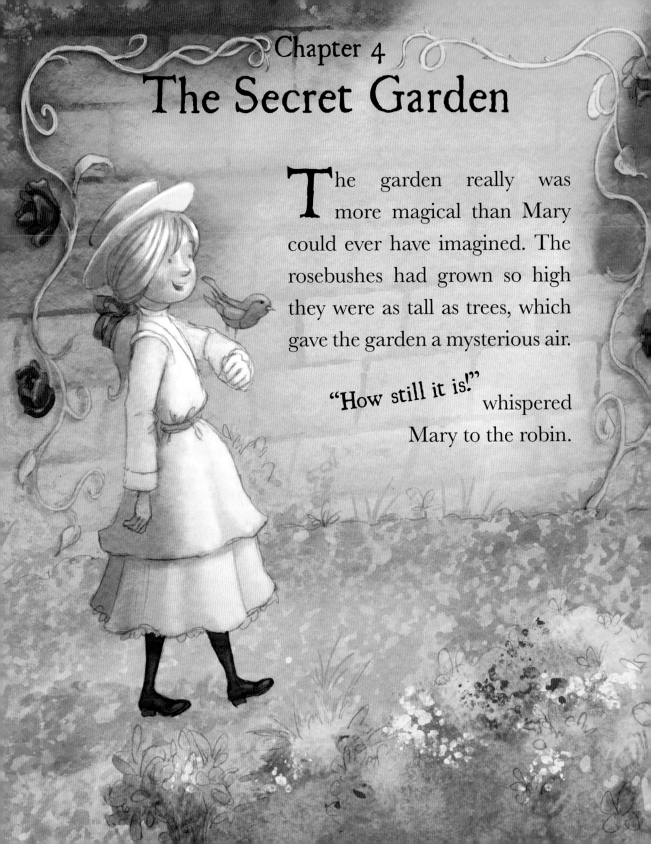

Chapter 4
The Secret Garden

The garden really was more magical than Mary could ever have imagined. The rosebushes had grown so high they were as tall as trees, which gave the garden a mysterious air.

"How still it is!" whispered Mary to the robin.

Mary wandered to and fro, clearing little patches of rough earth from some shoots that were trying to break through the ground.

Although not all of the rose's branches were in bloom, she could see signs of life everywhere. Now she just needed to help it come alive again!

Mary came up with a plan that very lunchtime. Martha had mentioned that her brother Dickon looked after animals on the moors and knew all about how things grew. Martha wrote him a letter.

Dear Dickon,

Miss Mary would like you to go to the shop in Thwaite for her. Please buy some gardening tools and seeds to make a flower bed.

Your loving sister,
Martha

A few days later, Mary found a boy playing a wooden whistle in one of the gardens while some rabbits and a squirrel sat close by – it was Dickon!

"Can you keep a secret?"

Mary asked Dickon.

"I've found Mrs Craven's secret garden."

To Mary's joy, Dickon loved the garden as much as she did.

"I'll help you bring this old place back to life!" he said.

That night, Mary woke with a start. She had definitely heard a person crying. This time she didn't care if Mrs Medlock told her off for exploring the old house.

Mary crept to the room hidden by the tapestry and went inside. There, she found a pale, crying boy, who gasped,
"Who are you? Are you a ghost?"
when he saw Mary.

"No, I'm Mary Lennox. Mr Craven is my uncle. Who are you?" she asked.

"Mr Craven is my father, so that means we are cousins," replied the boy. "I'm Colin Craven and I'm dying. My legs are too weak for me to stand on and no doctor can cure me."

Mary thought Colin didn't look like he was about to die, but she said nothing in case he started to cry again, and instead sat down and chatted to him.

"Perhaps you could come and see me again?" he asked hopefully when it was time for her to leave.

"Martha will keep our secret. She could tell you when it's safe to visit me."
Mary nodded and then crept back to bed.

From then on, Mary spent her days
either working alongside Dickon in
the secret garden, or with Colin.

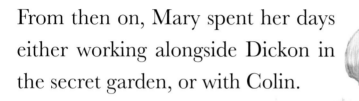

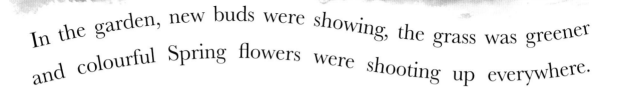

In the garden, new buds were showing, the grass was greener
and colourful Spring flowers were shooting up everywhere.

Colin asked Mary many questions about her life in India.
Before long, she had told him about the secret garden.
He hoped that if he ever became well enough,
he would be able to visit the garden too.

One day, Mrs Medlock found Mary in Colin's room, but before she could scold them, Colin said:

"I asked Mary to visit me.
She makes me feel better."

Mrs Medlock had no idea how this had come about, but Colin did look a little better.

Maybe Mary was doing the house some good after all!

Chapter 5
The Magic of the Garden

Because she was so busy gardening, some days Mary would forget to visit Colin. One day, he worked himself into a terrible rage.

"I won't let Dickon come here if you don't keep visiting me," snapped Colin.

"If you send Dickon away I shall **never** visit you again. You are a very selfish boy!" cried Mary.

"How **dare** you speak to me like that when I am dying?" raged Colin.

"You are not dying!" shouted Mary. "If you got some fresh air instead of lying in bed all day you'd be up and walking in no time!"

Nobody had ever spoken to Colin like that before. "Do you really think I could live to grow up?" he sobbed. "I should so like to meet Dickon and see the garden for myself."

"Yes," said Mary, gently. "I really do."

The next morning, Colin's nurse was surprised to see Mary throw his window wide open to let in some fresh air. Then Colin made an announcement.

"Nurse, I have invited a boy called Dickon to come and see me. He is going to bring some animals. Please show him up the moment he arrives."

And indeed, that morning Dickon did arrive, bringing with him a fox, a crow and two squirrels. He put a new-born lamb in Colin's arms and within minutes they were chatting like old friends.

Before long, the day came when Colin was carried by the strongest manservant downstairs and placed carefully in his wheelchair.

With Dickon pushing him, Colin took his first breaths of air outside. Together, they walked along the paths to the secret garden, making sure that no one followed them. They made Colin close his eyes.

Once they were inside and Mary had closed the door behind them, Colin opened his eyes. He looked in wonder at what Mary and Dickon had done.

Everywhere were splashes of pink, purple and white, with birds and butterflies flapping their pretty wings. The garden was truly magical.

Colin was overjoyed. He cried, "Mary! Dickon! I shall get well!"

"If you keep getting out in the fresh air, you'll be digging with us before too long," Dickon announced.

"Dig? Shall I?" cried Colin. "But my legs are so thin and weak! I am afraid to stand up on them."

"Once you get over being afraid, you'll stand on them alright," said Dickon firmly. "Just you see."

Suddenly, Colin said in a loud whisper,
"Who is that man?"

Ben Weatherstaff glared at them over
the top of the wall from a ladder.
"What are you doing in here?" he growled.
"And who is that?"

"I am Colin Craven, and this garden is mine to
do with as I please!" said Colin, grandly.

Ben spoke in a shaky voice. "You're Mrs Craven's boy?
I thought you couldn't get out of bed!"

Colin threw the blanket over his legs aside. Mary went pale and muttered under her breath, "He can do it! He can do it!"

She watched Colin hold out his arms to Dickon. Then his thin legs stretched out, his feet touched the ground and with that, Colin stood as tall and upright as any boy in Yorkshire.

"Look at me!" Colin cried out.

"See! My legs do work, they really do!"

"I am not afraid any more," said Colin, with great determination. "There is magic in here and it is making me strong."

Ben Weatherstaff had heard rumours that the boy was too sickly to even walk. Instead he was standing tall and proud before him. Ben scrambled down the ladder as quickly as he could.

Once inside, the gardener looked around with a smile and told Colin, "After your mother died, I came in over the wall once or twice a year to cut back the roses and keep some of the plants going."

Everyone was delighted that Ben had continued coming to the garden, and that he could keep a secret.

40

Together, they planted a rose in
Colin's mother's garden and as the
sun set on the day,

there Colin stood — on his own two feet — laughing.

Chapter 6
Home

The Summer months passed by in a flash, every day seeing Colin grow stronger. Colin, Mary, Dickon and Ben continued to work secretly in the garden. Mrs Medlock had no idea what was making Colin look so well, but she encouraged him to keep going outside with Mary, especially as there were no more tantrums or rudeness from either of them.

With Ben Weatherstaff's help, the garden flourished, just as it had when Colin's mother had tended to it. Drawn in by Dickon and his talent with animals, all sort of creatures made their home there.

It was paradise.

While the secret garden was coming alive, and two children were coming alive with it, Colin's father still grieved for his dead wife. He had spent all these years alone, travelling and mourning.

But one day, when he was wandering in a valley in the Austrian countryside, Mr Craven thought to himself,

"I almost feel as if I am alive!"

Later, he would discover that at that very moment in England, Colin had first gone into the garden and cried **"I shall get well!"**

One night soon after that, Colin's father heard his beloved wife's voice calling to him in a dream, saying,

"I am in the garden!"

In that moment,
Mr Craven knew he **had** to go home.

The ivy still hung thick over the wall, but the secret garden sounded alive as Mr Craven approached it. All at once, a sheet of ivy swung back and a boy ran through it and almost fell into his arms.

Mr Craven gasped,
"Who?
What?"

This was not the boy he remembered lying ill in bed.

Colin could scarcely believe his father was before him either! In a rush of words, he cried, **"Father, it's me, Colin! The garden has made me well. I am going to live!"**

Mr Craven and his son hugged properly for the first time in their lives. **"Take me into the garden, boy, and tell me all about it,"** said Mr Craven.

And so Colin led him inside to meet his niece Mary, and Dickon and Ben. There, they all sat together on the grass and told Mr Craven the story of how Mary's belief had made the garden, and Colin, alive again.

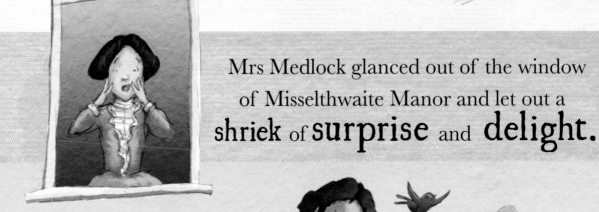

Mrs Medlock glanced out of the window of Misselthwaite Manor and let out a **shriek** of **surprise** and **delight**.

Across the lawn came Mr Craven, back from his travels at last. At his side was Colin, walking strongly and steadily. And skipping alongside them was Mary Lennox, the little girl whose magic had brought them all back to life.